Reader Books Weekly Reader Books

Weekly Reader Books presents

The Case of the Nervous Newsboy

A McGurk Mystery

By E. W. Hildick

ILLUSTRATED BY LISL WEIL

Macmillan Publishing Co., Inc.
New York

Copyright © 1976 E. W. Hildick
Illustrations copyright © 1976 Macmillan
Publishing Co., Inc.

Macmillan Publishing Co., Inc.
866 Third Avenue, New York, N.Y. 10022
Collier Macmillan Canada, Ltd.

Printed in the United States of America
This edition is published by arrangement with
Macmillan Publishing Co., Inc.

LIBRARY OF CONGRESS CATALOGING IN PUBLICATION DATA
Hildick, Edmund Wallace. The case of the nervous
newsboy. (A McGurk mystery)
Summary: Ten-year-old Jack McGurk and his
fellow detectives match wits with the local police
as they track down a runaway newsboy.
[1. Mystery and detective stories]
1. Weil, Lisl.   II. Title.
PZ7.H5463Cau   [Fic]   75-35873
ISBN 0-02-743790-6

Contents

Contents

1 The Shadow Squad

I guess it would have made anyone nervous.

The McGurk Special Foolproof Shadow Squad Plan is what I'm thinking about.

You see, it was the first time we had put it into operation, that very morning. It was only a training session, sure. But of course Simon didn't know that. To Simon—delivering his newspapers, minding his own business, all caught up with troubles of his own —it must have been pretty alarming.

But first, a word about this plan, and McGurk, and the rest of the Organization.

We specialize in detective work. Jack McGurk is the leader. His basement is where we have our headquarters. He thinks of himself as the "Brains" of the outfit. Sometimes I think the brightest thing about his head is the red hair that grows on it. But—well—I have to admit that he gets lots of good ideas. They seem to spring out along with his freckles—and that's a *very* large number.

But McGurk is not the only one with brains.

I am Joey Rockaway, the one who writes all the Organization's reports and makes notes and keeps records. Accurate reports. Careful notes. Complete records. And that takes regular, steady brainwork, believe me.

Wanda Grieg also has her share of good ideas. Sometimes, when it looks as if we are all baffled by a mystery and McGurk's bright ideas seem to die out like sparks, Wanda will come up with a truly brilliant suggestion.

Now Willie—no. Willie Sandowsky could never claim to be the "Brains" of any organization. The Nose—yes. In fact that is just what a lot of people actually do call him, and not just because his nose is the longest in the neighborhood. It is also the keenest and most sensitive. I still can't believe it's as keen and sensitive as Willie says it is, but I have to admit that it has helped to solve more than one mystery, one way or another.

Anyway, at the time I am writing about, the Organization seemed to have run out of cases. There was no mystery for any of our brains or noses to be working on. So, one Monday evening, McGurk called a meeting in his basement to spring the plan on us.

"Men," he said, "I have an idea. Just because business is slack, we can't let ourselves get rusty. It's time we had another training session."

"Oh, no!" cried Wanda, shaking her head so that her hair flew sideways and whipped Willie on the nose.

"No!" I said. "You can't catch us with *that* trick again, McGurk."

"No!" Willie growled, shaking his own head but taking care to stand well clear of Wanda this time. "No way!"

"What do you mean?" said McGurk. "Trick? What trick?"

"Like the *last* training session you dreamed up," said Wanda.

"Looking for clues in your yard," said Willie.

"Slaving away all morning, picking up trash," I said.

"And then finding out it was one of your weekend chores we'd been doing for you!"

McGurk gave us all a sad smile.

"But think of the practice it gave you. Think of how it sharpened your eyes for searching for real clues." He frowned. "Anyway, who said anything about clues this time? This time it's training for *shadowing*."

"Shadowing?"

We began to look and sound interested.

McGurk's eyes were gleaming. He reached under the long table that runs across the center of the basement. He pulled up a roll of paper.

"Yes," he said, slowly unfurling the roll. "The Mc-Gurk Foolproof Shadow Squad Plan." He clamped the edges of the paper down with the boxes we keep records and clues in. "I was working on this just before the meeting. Gather around."

He needn't have told us to do that. We were

gathered around long before he'd finished speaking. We were gathered around and staring at the diagrams he had drawn with a thick blue pencil.

"What's *that* supposed to be?" said Wanda.
"Who's this guy called 'Suspect?'" said Willie.

"*That*," said McGurk, "is the way we operate. *Suspect* is the guy we are shadowing."

"But—"

"In diagram A, Wanda and I are behind him, and Joey and Willie in front, on the opposite side."

"Yes, I can see that. But—"

"In diagram B, the suspect has turned the corner. Wanda and I are still behind, so we have him in sight. Joey and Willie, being in front, didn't know to turn right. But now they have stopped and are checking."

"McGurk, what is the point—?"

"The point is clear in diagram C. You and I, Wanda, have hurried on ahead of the suspect, on the opposite side. So now it is Willie and Joey's turn to follow him. At the next turning the same thing will happen and we switch positions again. And so on."

McGurk looked around sternly. Then he continued:

"That way we have him covered wherever he goes. And that way there is no risk of making him suspicious, which is how he'd be if he spotted the same people behind him all the time."

"Hmm—well," Wanda murmured, gazing down at the diagrams. "It certainly *looks* good."

"Uh—yeah!" Willie grunted. "I—I guess."

"But kind of complicated, don't you think, Mc-Gurk?" I said. I glanced at Willie. "For some of us?"

McGurk grinned.

"Sure," he said. "But that's where the training session comes in. Practice. By the time we've worked on it a few times it'll be just like walking the dog. Nothing to it."

Wanda looked at her watch. It was seven already.

"I guess I have another half-hour before I have to go home. If—"

"Huh-uh!"

McGurk was shaking his head.

"A plan like this needs to be practiced in the morning. When you're all fresh and alert. What I had in mind was for you all to copy out the three diagrams, take them home, study them. Study them last thing tonight, before you go to bed. Sleep with them under your pillow if you like. But get them so they're fixed in your mind, all ready to go in the morning."

Once again there was no need for him to give his instructions. We all know a good idea when we hear it. Even Willie.

I was busy handing out sheets of typing paper before McGurk was through speaking.

Well, all right.

I *still* think it's a good idea.

I still think it would work fine. In a busy downtown area. After a lot of practice.

But in a quiet neighborhood like ours, no.

For one thing, McGurk's plan requires many strange movements, especially in the diagram B stage. I mean all that dashing around when the two behind have to run on in front. Or when the dummy in front of the first pair forgets to stop and check the situation after the first turning, and has to be yelled at to come on back and take up the rear position. Or when the leader of the squad can't resist turning and waving at the rest like a red-haired maniac—trying to get them to close up, or fall back, or walk with their heads down, or pretend to blow their noses, or whatever.

I mean in a busy downtown area, all this movement and noise gets lost in the general bustle. The suspect never becomes alerted to the fact that he's being shadowed.

But on *our* quiet streets and avenues. . . .

Then too, that same quietness made even practicing almost impossible. There just didn't seem to be anyone around to practice *on*.

No, the place wasn't deserted. People were going off to work. But in *cars*. Every single one of them in a car. And the best shadow squad in the business is no good without wheels, if the suspect is driving along at twenty-five miles an hour.

And sure, there were one or two little kids around who *were* on foot. But who wants to shadow Sue Gallo and her lousy Teddy Bear, when you know for a fact she's on her way to visit Marni Williams and her crummy dolls to pretend they're running a day care center?

I tell you, we were so desperate we were just looking around for a dog to shadow, when along came Simon Emmet with his bike and his sack of papers.

"All right, men," murmured McGurk. "We'll take him. Forget that we know who he is. Assume he's an enemy agent, and the sack's full of secret missile plans."

2 Simon Rides Away

Simon Emmet was nervous to begin with, even before the Shadow Squad got to work. I can see that now.

Usually, he was very calm and orderly. For instance, he never used to throw his newspapers onto the porches, the way some newsboys do. You know: not bothering to see if the papers have landed safely, never getting off their bikes from one end of the route to the other. That sort of thing.

No. Simon was a model newsboy. He gave himself plenty of time. He studied the weather. If it looked like rain, he came prepared, with an extra cape to throw over the papers to make sure they arrived dry. And, rain or shine, he folded them neatly and placed them in the mailboxes as carefully as if they were eggs or fragile china. What's more, although he never rushed through his work, he wasn't slow either. Just nice and steady and thoughtful.

Usually.

On this particular morning, though, things were different. As we watched him come down the street, it seemed as if he really was an enemy agent with a sackful of top secrets.

He kept stopping and frowning, staring down at his shoes and shaking his head. Then, as if remem-

bering to try to act naturally and get on with his delivering without wasting time, he would dive into his bag and pull out a paper and start up a driveway with it. Then he'd become nervous again and twist that folded paper as he approached the mailbox and stuff it in any old way. Then back down the driveway he would dart toward his bike and his sack—only stopping on the way still another time to frown and shake his head.

Now, as I said, this had nothing to do with us. He hadn't even *seen* us yet. We were behind the bushes in McGurk's front yard, waiting for the order to go. And we didn't pay much attention to this strange behavior right then. We were more concerned with how the plan would work out, using Simon as the suspect for our training session.

Wanda was the first to doubt it—with Simon still about ten houses away.

"This is stupid!" she said. "We know where *he's* going."

"Yeah," said Willie. "Even I can tell you which street he'll turn into next. And I haven't lived here long."

"I know that!" said McGurk. "But this is just *practice*. This is just to see if we can do it correctly,

according to the plan. And if we can do it without making him suspicious."

"He looks—" I began.

But McGurk cut me short. His eyes were gleaming again.

"Don't forget. For this exercise, old Simon's an

enemy agent. Armed. Desperate. And if he does notice us in particular—we're *dead!*"

That was different. All of us—Wanda, Willie and me—shut up and tensed up. McGurk has this way of making you believe in his fantasies, and the way he said that—"If he notices . . . we're dead"—sent a shiver down *my* back.

In fact I think it made us tense up *too* much. Must have. Because when Simon had reached the house two doors away and McGurk sent Willie and me off to take up our positions across the street, everything started going wrong.

Willie walked jerkily, as if his legs were in steel splints. To try and mask this unnatural gait, I closed in behind him so that I was breathing down his neck. This startled him so much that he gave a little yelp that I'm sure Simon must have heard, though I didn't dare look back. Then Willie stepped up the pace to widen the gap and overdid it—jerking along in big strides that would have left both the suspect and the rest of the squad miles behind, if I hadn't grabbed his shirt.

Then he yelped again and came to a dead stop, so that I stumbled into him and we both nearly went down and I had to look back.

Sure enough, the "suspect" was staring at us. He was standing still again next to his bike, but staring at us rather than his feet. Then he swiveled around to where McGurk and Wanda had taken up their positions, farther along, behind him. Since Simon had stopped, they had stopped too. McGurk was looking up at a roof, pretending to study a blue jay like it was a golden eagle. Wanda was putting on a similar act, only with her it was a weed growing at the base of a tree. She made like it was a rare wild orchid or something.

"All right!" said Simon, in a hard, gritty voice.

McGurk went on with his bird-watching. The way he was squinting now it was as if the golden eagle had started to lay red, white, and blue eggs.

Wanda went on with her botanizing, acting like she'd just spotted three more wild orchids.

"*All right!*" said Simon again, even louder, swiveling back to Willie and me.

I would have done my best to brave it out, pretending not to hear. My instinct was to put my hands in my pockets, start whistling, and go strolling along. But Willie. . . .

He had to answer back.

"Hi, Simon!" he said, blushing to the tip of his

nose and giving a sickly grin. "I guess you spotted us, huh?"

"You're darned right I spotted you!" growled Simon, marching straight up to Willie and grabbing a handful of his shirt. "So what's it all about, huh? Come on! The truth! I want to know!"

Willie's grin faded, and no wonder.

Simon's normally smooth, brown, peaceful face was all twisted. His usually neat dark hair was tumbling into his eyes. He was annoyed, upset, scared, jumpy, suspicious—and it all showed.

"I—huh—we—we were just shadowing—kind of—yeah—shadowing you is all, Simon!"

"Hah! I can see that! I could tell that! Oh, sure!" He went on shaking Willie by the shirt.

"Hey, take it easy, Simon!"

This was McGurk. And let me say right here and now that whatever his faults, the head of the Organization never deserts his men when they're in trouble.

"Hah! *You!*" Simon removed his hand from Willie's shirt and switched it to McGurk's. "You and your crummy detective outfit, huh? You hiring yourself out to spy on other kids now, huh?"

"I—"

"Don't lie! I know. I see what she's—arrgh! You make me *sick!*"

And with that, Simon—the quiet, orderly, peaceful, thoughtful Simon Emmet, who always treated us with respect, even though he was three years older—gave McGurk a shove that sent him spinning into me and Wanda, nearly knocking the girl over.

"What—what's gotten into *him?*" murmured McGurk, gaping after the newsboy.

"He—look—he's *riding* away!" I said. "He's leaving out the rest of the street!"

"Wow!" gasped Willie. "We made a mess of that! We *are* dead!"

"Yes, but I don't understand," said Wanda. "I've never see him like that. Ever."

"He seemed to think it was you," said McGurk, turning to look at her. "He said something about 'she'—"

"No," I said. "I don't think he meant Wanda. I

was watching. He didn't even glance at her. He was too busy glaring at you, McGurk."

Wanda was still looking dazed. Her eyes were fixed on the corner which the newsboy had just turned, pedaling like mad, out of sight.

"Simon Emmet, though. . . . Behaving like that! I—I just can't believe it!"

Well, as I said at the beginning, I suppose it was no wonder the newsboy should be nervous, after tangling with the Shadow Squad.

But not *that* nervous.

Not so nervous that he didn't finish his morning deliveries.

Not so nervous that he didn't go home for lunch.

Not so nervous that he didn't show for his afternoon paper route.

And certainly not so nervous that he didn't even turn up at bedtime.

You see, that was the day that Simon Emmet disappeared.

Completely.

Without a trace.

So that even the police couldn't find him.

3 Key Witnesses

We didn't get to hear about his disappearance until the following morning.

Simon lived about a half mile away from us, and it was vacation time. So it wasn't as if we could get to know the latest from kids at school who did live near him.

But Wanda's mother was a good friend of Mrs. Emmet's, and Mrs. Emmet told her all about it early Wednesday morning.

Wanda came bursting into McGurk's basement with the news.

"Hey! Guess what! I—"

"You're late!" said McGurk. "This is the day we're

all going downtown, remember? This is the day we pick ourselves a complete stranger, in a busy street, and shadow him from there. A *real* training session. And you're more than a half-hour late."

"I was detained on official business," said Wanda, folding her arms and finishing with a sniff.

"What do you mean, *official* business? What's more official than a real full-scale training session?"

"Learning the facts about a real full-scale mystery," said Wanda. "Concerning someone we were all talking to only yesterday." She sniffed again. "But of course if you'd rather we hurried on to this terribly important training sess—"

"Who? What mystery?" asked McGurk.

"You mean Simon Emmet?" I said.

"Yes."

"Joey," said McGurk, who knows about putting first things first, "get ready to take notes."

"Did you find out why he was acting the way he was?" asked Willie.

"No," said Wanda. "That's still a mystery. But an even bigger mystery is where he's vanished to. His mother's going crazy with worry. . . ."

Then she told us about how Simon had not shown for lunch or supper and had been missing all night.

As she was speaking, I was busy getting it all down in my notebook.

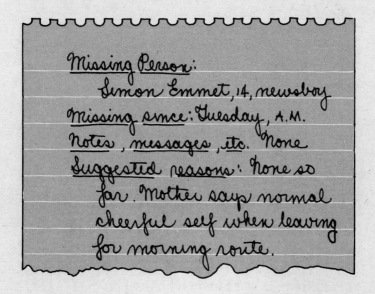

Missing Person:
   Simon Emmet, 14, newsboy
Missing since: Tuesday, A.M.
Notes, messages, etc. None
Suggested reasons: None so
far. Mother says normal
cheerful self when leaving
for morning route.

"Well he wasn't his normal cheerful self when he met up with *us*," said McGurk.

"You can say that again!" said Willie, nervously fingering his shirt.

"So something must have bugged him between leaving home and meeting us," I said. "Because it certainly wasn't us."

"No, we weren't *that* bad!" said Wanda, sadly.

We others could guess what she was thinking. When McGurk put it into words, we all agreed.

"Gee!" he sighed. "I wish he'd have told *us* about it."

And this wasn't just because we'd have been glad for something to do. It was mainly because of the way we felt about Simon himself.

"He was a real nice kid," I said. "Always ready to help others. I remember once when I was fishing in the park. I'd got the line all tangled up in some bushes. I thought I'd have to cut it and leave it. Then Simon came along and spent nearly an hour helping me free it."

"Yes," said Wanda. "He was like that. Three years ago, when I was only seven and I'd just started to climb trees, it was Simon who rescued me."

"*You?* Stuck up a tree?" asked McGurk, as surprised as I was. I mean Wanda's *the* best tree climber in the whole neighborhood. Somehow we'd always imagined her being able to swing and clamber among the branches almost as soon as she could walk, like that son of Tarzan's.

"No," said Wanda, blushing slightly. "It was worse than that. I—I fell off. It was only from about four feet up. But I was just a little kid and the shock made me cry. Then Simon came up and told me not to worry. 'You go right back up that old tree, honey,' he said. 'Right now. Go on. I'll give you a leg up.' And he did, and I did, and I guess it was like with Army pilots when they crash. If they don't go up again right away, they get scared for life."

"Even me," said Willie. "Yeah. Even me, and I've only lived around here a couple of months. But when I got lost over the other side of the park that first week, Simon saw me, and recognized me, and he could see I was getting panicky. So you know what he did? He took time off from his route to escort me back to where I knew where I was."

"And I remember the time when he—"

McGurk broke off. His face suddenly got very red. It must have been a very embarrassing memory.

"Mind you," he said. "I was *very* little at the time and—"

He shook his head. It was obviously too delicate a subject even to mention.

Then he looked up and glared at us, as we waited, hanging on every word.

"Anyway, what is this? A *wake?* The guy's missing, not dead."

"Well, we *hope* not dead. But—"

"But he could have used our help and we didn't give it to him. We! The McGurk Organization. Well we can start fixing that, right here and now."

"How?"

"By investigating the mystery, that's how."

"The police are doing that," said Wanda. "Mrs. Emmet told my mother—"

"Then we'll help the police," said McGurk. "We'll put our Organization at their—their—"

"Disposal?" I said.

"Yeah. At their dispersal. I mean we must have

been the last people around here to *see* Simon. I mean you know what that makes us? It makes us key witnesses."

I liked the sound of that. I was just writing it down in my notebook when Wanda cut in.

"Sure it does. That's what I told my mother. She went straight back to the phone and told Mrs. Emmet. And Mrs. Emmet said she'd let the police know right away and would I stay home until they came."

"And did you?" asked Willie.

"No. I said we all saw Simon at the same time. I said the best thing would be for me to come around here and for them to talk to us all together. Right?"

"Good thinking, Officer Grieg," said McGurk, very gravely.

You could see that the idea of a visit from the police, in his own headquarters, was getting to him in a big way.

Then he clapped his hands.

"Right, men! We have to do this thing 100 percent correct. They'll probably send a real big wheel on a case like this. Captain at least. And we have to show them."

"Show them?" Willie looked around. "Show them what?"

"Show them we're not just any old witnesses. We're—well, we're different. We're like professionals. We'll have to have all our facts ready. Neat. Crisp. One-two-three. . . . Joey, get this down. Now. Straight onto the typewriter. Ready?"

In about thirty seconds I was. And at the end of another two minutes I had typed, at McGurk's dictation, the following:

STATEMENT

We, the undersigned (members of the McGurk Organization, Private Investigators), last saw Simon Emmet at approximately 8:30 A.M. last Tuesday morning. He was

And that's as far as I had gotten when there was this brisk knock at the outer door that led up into the yard.

"*I'll* get that!" said McGurk, grabbing Willie with one hand and Wanda with the other.

Then:

"No," he said, changing his mind and going back to the rocking chair behind the table. "I bet the captain doesn't go to open *his* office door. You get it, Willie. Show him in. And straighten your shoulders. And remember to say 'sir.' "

So Willie went, almost falling backward in his effort to straighten his shoulders. And he did say "sir." In fact he kept on saying it, all the time he was opening the door.

"Sir . . . will you . . . sir . . . please . . . *sir?*"

Well, it was a policeman, all right.

But it wasn't a captain. It wasn't a lieutenant either. It was not even a sergeant. It was just an elderly patrolman. Patrolman Cassidy. The one who comes around the schools to check bikes and talk about road safety:

"Hi!" he said, pushing his hat to the back of his gray head and grinning down at Willie. "I hear you might have some information for us, young man."

4 Patrolman Cassidy

When we saw it was only Patrolman Cassidy we were disappointed. Three of us were, anyway. But the fourth—the one who'd been doing all the talking about captains and lieutenants—acted as if Patrolman Cassidy was the one person in the world he most wanted to see.

"Hey!" cried McGurk, getting up from his chair and leaving it rocking wildly. "This *is* a surprise. Welcome to my office, Mr. Cassidy. Meet my staff."

Note that. "*My*" office. "*My*" staff. The chance to show off to *any* outsider was enough to cheer McGurk up. And after all, this was a real policeman.

"Ha! It's you, young M'Turk!" said Patrolman

Cassidy cheerfully. (He'd glanced at the notice on the door, but not quite carefully enough to get the name right.) "Nice place you got here."

"Sure," said McGurk. "Take a seat, Mr. Cassidy. Here. . . ."

And the jerk gave the policeman *my* chair.

Patrolman Cassidy took it. He peered at the paper in the typewriter and grunted.

"See you been working on this already, young Mc—" he peered closer—"Gurk. Yeah. . . . Organization, huh? Private Investigators. . . . Well now—"

"Sure thing, officer!" said McGurk, sitting up straight and smirking broadly at the visitor. "That's us. We—"

"You got a license, of course?" said the patrolman, looking up from the half-finished statement.

That took McGurk's smirk away.

"License?"

"Yeah. All private investigators have to be licensed, you know."

"Oh . . . well . . . sure. We—we're working on that. But we do have ID cards. Men!"

As McGurk took out his card, he gave us a look to tell us to do the same.

Mr. Cassidy seemed very impressed by the four

cards being waved in front of his face. And no wonder. I mean I'd done a good job typing those cards, with all our descriptions and details and so on. Besides, each card had a photograph of its holder, with a complete set of fingerprints.

"Hey! Those look real official. You know that?"

McGurk seemed ready to burst with pride.

Coming from a real cop, that was high praise. In fact, I wouldn't have been surprised if McGurk had gone on to ask to see Mr. Cassidy's card, just to compare it to ours and maybe pick up a few fancy ideas.

But as I said earlier, with McGurk it's first things first. He became all serious.

"You came about Simon Emmet?" he asked, leaning back a little.

"Ah, yes . . . that." Mr. Cassidy looked a bit more serious too. "Yes. I understand you were some of the last to see him around. Want to tell me about it?"

McGurk pointed to the half-finished statement and began:

"Well, we were just—"

But the patrolman cut him short.

"In your own words will be fine. Just nice and natural. Leaving nothing out."

McGurk nodded.

"Well—" He paused. "Aren't you going to take notes, officer?"

Mr. Cassidy grinned.

"At this stage, no. Why don't we just have a chat about it? Like I say—nice and easy, huh? People always seem to recall things better this way. Wave a notebook and pencil at them and they kinda dry up."

"Hear that, McGurk?" said Wanda, triumphantly. "You're always getting Joey here to wave his notebook at people and—"

"Yes, well," said Mr. Cassidy. "There is a time for that, and I'm sure young McWhirter here knows all about it."

McGurk's scowl for Officer Grieg turned into a beam for Officer Cassidy. The patrolman could have misnamed him McJerk for all he cared after *that* comment.

"Sure," he said. "You bet. . . . Well, it happened like this. We were having a training session yesterday morning. . . ."

And so, with occasional interruptions from the rest of us, McGurk told the policeman of our encounter with Simon.

The cop sat back with his legs crossed, playing with the visor of his hat where it was hung over his knee. He did a good deal of nodding and grunting, but otherwise made no comment until McGurk was through.

Then he showed why *he* could manage without a notebook. Years and years of training and experience. Right away he picked on the most important points.

"Did he say *what* had been bugging him?"

We looked at one another, trying to remember.

"Besides *yourselves*, that is," said Mr. Cassidy, in a low, encouraging sort of voice.

"He—he did mention a 'she,'" said Wanda. "I remember, because first I thought he might have

meant me. Then I saw he wasn't even looking at me."

The policeman nodded.

"Good," he said. "You train your staff well, McGurk." (This time he got it right.) "Now. Think carefully, all of you. What were his exact words?"

"Well—he kind of only mentioned it," said McGurk. "Just—she—she—"

"A half-finished sentence," I said. "Something like: 'I know what she's—' Or: 'I see what she's—' Then finish. Nothing else."

"Huh—in what connection would that be?"

"Well—hold it!" McGurk squeezed his eyes shut. "Yes. Just after he'd accused us of spying on him."

"Hiring ourselves out to spy on him," said Wanda.

"Yes," said Willie. "And there was a smell, too. . . ."

But he spoke so low and uncertainly that no one took much notice.

Mr. Cassidy was nodding at Wanda and McGurk.

"Yes. Well now, that doesn't surprise me. You sure he didn't mention anyone by name? His mother, for instance?"

We shook our heads.

"You think he meant her?" asked McGurk.

Officer Cassidy shrugged.

"Could have. Usually when a kid runs away from home, it's after a run-in with his parents, you know."

We knew. There wasn't one of us who hadn't planned such a move, at one time or another. It figured.

"Especially with her really being his stepmother and all," said the policeman.

We didn't know *that*. At least none of us boys did.

"Is that right?" McGurk asked Wanda.

"Oh—yes. Sure. I thought you knew. Sorry. His real mother died a few years ago. This one married his father last year. But she and Simon get along fine."

McGurk didn't look so sure. I think the word "stepmother" had started something in that suspicious mind of his.

He turned to Mr. Cassidy.

"Does *she* say she had a fight with him?" he asked.

Mr. Cassidy gave him a fierce look. Then relaxed.

"Well, normally *we* ask the questions, not the witnesses. But seeing as you're kind of in the same business and all—why, no. Mrs. Emmet didn't say there'd been a fight of any kind. But then, parents don't always know when they have been in a fight with their kids. They just lay down the rules, and sometimes a high-spirited boy or girl will object, but the parent won't listen. To the *parent* it isn't a fight—but to the kid it really is."

We nodded. I was thinking: No wonder they send Patrolman Cassidy around the schools. He really *understands*. . . .

"Anyway," he went on, "assuming it is the usual —any of you know if he has any special hideouts?"

We didn't. We had to admit it. Simon didn't live near enough for us to have found out such things for ourselves. And we were too young for him ever to have confided in us about matters like that.

"Oh, well—I guess it isn't all that important," said Patrolman Cassidy, putting on his hat and standing up. "He'll turn up, soon as he's hungry enough. Thank you for your—"

"One minute, sir." McGurk had stood up, too, ready to escort him to the door. "Are we still key witnesses? I mean—were we really the last to see him?"

"Key witnesses? Well now, I guess you could say that—being so reliable and all. And—yes—I guess you could say you were *among* the last to see him."

"Who else was there? When? Sir . . . ?"

Patrolman Cassidy grinned.

"O.K.," he said. "You deserve to be answered

straight, after all your straight answers. There was one person saw him around 9:45. A mailman. Said a boy of that description was hanging around Central Boulevard at Weaver. Looked like he was trying to hitch a ride downtown. We're working on that angle, too."

At the door, Wanda put the next question.

"Mr. Cassidy, you don't think anything—well—*bad*—has happened to Simon, do you?"

The policeman laughed.

"No, no, honey! I tell you—this is all normal, so far. It happens all the time."

"So far, yes," said Wanda. "But if—"

"Well, if he doesn't show by suppertime *today*, yes. Then the search will get more intensive."

"More *intensive?*" asked McGurk.

"That means—" I began.

"It means more men will be deployed," said the policeman, beginning to look grave. "There'll be a statewide alarm. And there'll probably be a special team put on the job, with a Field HQ."

"What's a Field HQ?" asked McGurk, pouncing on that phrase on the steps of his own HQ.

"A place for the men to meet and change shifts and maybe sift statements and evidence and—"

"Hey! You could use *this!* Our HQ. Why don't you? Please! Be my—our guests!"

"That's very kind of you," said Mr. Cassidy. "And the Chief would be much obliged for your offer, I'm sure. But we have a specially equipped trailer for the job. Anyway—" He laughed again. "It won't come to that, I'm sure. Soon as Simon gets hungry, you'll be seeing him again."

But as we watched the elderly patrolman amble

down the path to his car—stopping to stroke the neighbors' cat—we weren't so sure.

"Some kids, yes," said McGurk. "Most kids, maybe. But Simon just doesn't seem the sort to run away over a little fight."

"And the way he was acting, it had been more than a little fight," said Wanda.

"And I bet if Simon did run away, he'd run away!" said Willie.

We looked at him.

"I mean really make a good job of it. Like his paper deliveries."

We nodded.

"But that doesn't mean he couldn't get into serious trouble," said Wanda. "I mean—staying out *all night!*"

"You're right," said McGurk. "The official police are treating this too lightly. They don't know Simon like we do. So . . . ."

We waited, as McGurk stood there, his eyes beginning to gleam again.

"So—what?"

"So we get to work ourselves. Right now. Let's go, men!"

And he led the way back into *our* Field HQ.

5 Questions—
and a Few Answers

I don't know whether it was because we were competing with the real police, or because we thought such a lot about Simon. But McGurk was certainly on his toes.

The first thing he did, after Mr. Cassidy had left, was get me to write down some questions. Here they are:

1. Was there any argument, between Simon and his stepmother, Tuesday morning?
2. Was there any argument on Monday or Sunday?
3. Did Simon leave his bike or take it with him?
4. Did he take any money (big money, like savings) with him?

"What's the point in getting Joey to write them down?" asked Wanda, a bit scornfully.

"Because," said McGurk, taking the notebook and tearing off the page, "I want you to take them home and find the answers."

"Me?" said Wanda. "Why me?"

"Because we can't go bugging Mrs. Emmet with questions ourselves. Even if I was sure where she lives. But we can get to know through your mother, Wanda. She probably knows some of the answers already anyway. O.K.?"

"Oh—yes—sure!" said Wanda, no longer scornful.

"All right then," said McGurk. "So what are you waiting for? This is urgent, Officer Grieg!"

When Wanda had left, I asked McGurk about some of those questions.

"I can see why you want to check up about any argument," I said. "But what's this about the bike? And the money? I mean, about the bike, the mailman said he'd seen Simon trying to hitch a ride. He wouldn't have been doing that if he'd had his bike."

McGurk was so much on his toes, he didn't waste any time asking me who was the Brains of the outfit *now*.

"The mailman only said he'd seen someone *answering Simon's description*," he replied. "So he wasn't 100 percent sure. Well, a good detective organization *has* to be, and this way we'll find out. If Simon did take his bike, we'll know the mailman was probably wrong about the hitching."

"Gee! You're *right*, McGurk!" said Willie.

"O.K.," I said. "I see about the bike. But what about the money?"

"Easy," said McGurk. "If we know how much Simon took with him, we'll know how far he was planning to go. And for how long."

I had to agree. McGurk really was in top form. It seemed to be catching, too. At least it seemed to do something for Willie.

"Hey, and there might be a clue in that smell!"

We stared at him. Vaguely, I remembered him mentioning something about a smell earlier.

"What smell?" asked McGurk.

"Yesterday," said Willie. "You know."

"No, I don't know," said McGurk. "What smell yesterday?"

"On Simon," said Willie. "When he got mad and picked on me and grabbed my shirt. I got a real good snootful, I can tell you!"

"So?" said McGurk, who has greater faith in Willie's nose than I have. "What was it? And why didn't you say so before?"

"I tried to," said Willie. "But no one would listen. Maybe if you had and I'd tried to describe it *then*—well. . . . Maybe I'd have been able to name it."

"What d'you mean?" said McGurk. "You either smelled something or you didn't."

"Oh, I smelled something all right!" said Willie. "Yes, *sir!* But—well—I just can't put a name to it."

"Willie! This could be important! You *must* know what it was! With *your* nose!"

Willie shook his head. He looked very sad. His nose seemed longer than ever as he stroked its sharp end.

"I—I know it's the most sensitive nose in the world," he said. "I know it can pick up scents that most humans couldn't. But—but—"
He looked all set to burst into tears as his eyes turned from McGurk to me and back to McGurk.

"But my memory—it's just an ordinary rotten human memory—and I can't remember what the smell is *called!*"

"Would you know it if we said it?" asked McGurk.

"Yes, yes. . . ." moaned Willie. "But—"

"Some kind of food?" asked McGurk.

"Huh-uh!"

"Some kind of drink?" I asked.

"Huh-uh!"

"A chemical smell?"

"No—no—oh gosh—it's—it's on the tip of my nose!"

"Oh yeah?" said McGurk, leaning forward.

"No, not *really!*" howled Willie. "I mean like when you say some word's on the tip of your tongue. This smell's on the tip of my nose."

"In that case," I said, speaking as the word expert, "the best thing to do is to try not to think about it. Then it'll come naturally."

"Yes," said McGurk. "Forget it, Willie. It's probably not all that important anyway. . . . But this *could* be."

He was referring to Wanda, who had just opened the door, the list of questions in her hand.

"You got the answers?"

Wanda smiled proudly.

"All of them."

We gathered around to examine the answers she'd scribbled down.

No. There had definitely been no argument on Tuesday morning.

No. There had definitely been no arguments on Monday or Sunday, either. Or at any time in recent weeks, for that matter.

No. Simon had not taken his bike. He had dumped it in the back yard of his house, along with the undelivered papers.

"So the mailman was right," I said. "It *was* Simon who was trying to hitch a ride."

"Not necessarily," said McGurk.

"But you said—"

"I said it would probably have been Simon. But the answer to the money question makes me wonder if it could have been, after all."

The answer to the money question was No. Mrs. Emmet didn't think Simon could have taken much with him. His savings were in a special bank account, and he hadn't gone to draw them out.

"And she also checked on the household money," said Wanda. "Not that she thought Simon would ever steal from that. But anyway, it was all there."

McGurk was nodding thoughtfully.

"If he'd left the bike and taken the money, I'd have said he was counting on going a long way. Like Clark Timperley when he ran away last year. Hitching as far as New York so as not to leave a clear trail. Then taking a Greyhound bus up into New Hampshire."

"So?"

"So the chances are that Simon's hiding out locally someplace. Just the way Mr. Cassidy figured."

"A friend's house?"

"Huh-uh. The police will have covered that angle. No. Some kind of private hideout. A vacant house, maybe. Some outbuilding. Maybe in the woods at the edge of town. Personally, I'd say someplace he's noticed on his paper route. An empty house."

McGurk didn't need to say any more.

"Let's get our bikes!" I said.

"Right!" said Wanda.

"I know an empty house!" said Willie.

"But we'll do this thoroughly," said McGurk. "Street by street. With me directing."

And that is just what we did. Covering Simon's route, street by street, with McGurk directing us to look into this empty house and that vacant lot, peering into outbuildings and poking into masses of undergrowth. Sometimes it got us into trouble—like when we found a party of builders drinking beer and playing cards in an old shed. Or when we peered through the curtainless windows of what looked like an empty house, only to frighten a lady who was scrubbing the floor.

Simon, we found no trace of. But we did discover one thing as the afternoon wore on.

The police were not taking it as coolly as Patrolman Cassidy had pretended.

We noticed no fewer than three different patrol cars cruising around.

We saw policemen knocking on doors.

We even almost bumped into a couple of cops in the overgrown backyard of one of the empty houses. They were prodding the bushes with long sticks.

"Hi!" said McGurk, strutting forward with his ID card half out of his pocket.

"You kids know you're trespassing?" was all the reply he got.

We took the hint and left at once. Even McGurk didn't stay to argue after *that* cold reception.

No. Whatever Mr. Cassidy had tried to make us believe in the morning, the police pressure seemed to be building up in the afternoon.

And the evening paper underlined this fact.

"Take a look at *this!*" said McGurk.

He'd picked it up from where it had been tossed onto the front porch by Simon's substitute, Leo Johnson, the newsdealer's son.

"There was never a newsboy as careful as Simon," said Wanda sadly.

"No—I mean *this!*" said McGurk, slapping the front page.

He meant the story printed there, which I clipped for our own files. Here is the beginning:

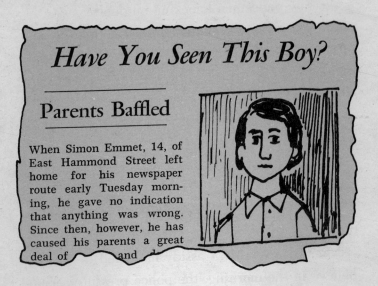

Have You Seen This Boy?

Parents Baffled

When Simon Emmet, 14, of East Hammond Street left home for his newspaper route early Tuesday morning, he gave no indication that anything was wrong. Since then, however, he has caused his parents a great deal of

Most of the rest is what I have already reported. One extra detail, though, was the mention of Simon's father.

Mr. Emmet had been on a business trip to Seattle, it said. When he heard of Simon's disappearance, he immediately started back.

McGurk was particularly interested in this. He had me read it out twice.

"What's so special about that?" asked Wanda.

"Well, nothing really," he murmured, his eyes in thoughtful green slits. "Except—well—except if Simon *did* take off on a long journey. That might just have been where he was heading."

"Where?" said Willie.

"Seattle," said McGurk. "To see his father. If the reason he ran away was serious enough—well. Maybe he figured that his father was the only one who could handle it."

"It's beginning to look very serious *now*, anyway!"

Wanda was pointing to another interesting bit at the end of the report:

Foul Play?

A tri-state alarm has now been put out. This is a routine measure in such cases and does not necessarily mean that Simon is considered to be in danger.

A police spokesman said today: "As of this time, we do not suspect foul play. If the boy does not return home soon, however, we shall have to take all appropriate steps to intensify the search."

"What—what's foul play?" whispered Willie.

"Dirty work!" snapped McGurk.

"You know," said Wanda. "Like kidnapping, robbery. . . ."

"Maybe even murder," I found myself mumbling.

Wanda looked again at the report. Her face was as pale and grim as mine felt. She stabbed a finger at what the police spokesman had said—about stepping up the search.

"I wonder how soon is 'soon'?" she said.

We found out—soon.

The very next morning, in fact.

Kidnapping

6 The Command Post

"Ah—ah—it's—ah—arrived!"

Willie came panting into our HQ shortly after 9:00 that Thursday morning.

"He *has?*" said McGurk. "When?"

"No—ah—not *he*. Not Simon. Ah—ah—*it!* It's arrived. I've just been to the supermarket, and it's there. On that vacant lot."

"*What* has?"

"The police thing. The whatsit. You know—"

"The trailer?"

"Yeah. The one that Mr. Cassidy told us about. And golly! You should see the size of it!"

We did see the size of it. In the next few minutes. And it wasn't only curiosity that had us hurrying along there. It was the feeling that if Willie had been correct, then things were beginning to look very grim for Simon. Very grim indeed.

Well, Willie had made no mistake. The trailer was a dark blue one, with the police department sign painted along the side, and it really was huge. It seemed to fill one-half of that vacant lot—while the other half was taken up by a couple of patrol cars and a police truck. Some men in uniform were busy carrying armfuls of equipment out of the truck and into the trailer—stacks of paper, clipboards, two-way radios, a bundle of long shiny sticks, a bunch of rubber boots. And spades. . . .

There were also other men in coveralls running out a reel of cord from the top of the trailer to a telephone pole. And Patrolman Cassidy was there, too, just standing at the foot of the steps leading to the trailer door.

"Is this it?" asked McGurk, going straight up to him.

"Oh, it's you, M'Turk," said the patrolman, squinting down. He wasn't looking so relaxed this time. "Yup. This is the Field HQ I was telling you about.

Or the Command Post, as Lieutenant Kaspar likes to call it."

"Does this mean you think there's been—er—foul play?" asked Wanda, gulping a little.

Mr. Cassidy tried to grin, but you could see it came hard.

"Well—I wouldn't say *that*, honey. Not exactly. Just routine is really what—"

"Cassidy, I thought I told you to keep all rubber-neckers away from here! Especially kids."

We stared up at the man who had just flung open the trailer door. There was no need for Mr. Cassidy to tell us who this was. He was wearing a gold lieutenant's shield, and the eyes in that tight-skinned shiny pink face were a very fierce flashing blue.

"The dogs'll be here in about an hour," he said to the patrolman, "and I want you to—"

"Dogs?"

This was McGurk who had interrupted, eager green eyes flashing up at the fierce blue ones.

The lieutenant scowled.

"You still here? Now I'll tell you one more time and once only. As of this morning, this lot is police property and—"

"That's all right, Lieutenant. These are the kids I

told you about. The ones who were among the last to see the boy."

"So?" said the lieutenant, sweeping us with those eyes, then flashing back at the patrolman. "They have something to add to their statement?"

"Well no, but I guess they're just eager to help and—"

"Sure, sure! But right now we're too busy. So move it, you four. You hear?"

"But we *do* have something to add, Lieutenant," said McGurk.

I looked at Wanda and Willie, and they looked at me.

It was our "Oh-oh, here we go!" look.

Because we knew for a fact that McGurk did *not* have something to add.

Or at least we thought we knew.

"Make it snappy then!" said the lieutenant.

"Well, mentioning dogs did it," said McGurk, looking very pleased with himself.

And we all looked at each other again.

This time it was with our "What's he got up his sleeve *this* time?" look.

"Dogs?" said the lieutenant.

"Yeah," said McGurk. "Sniffing things out. Well

let me tell you, Lieutenant, Willie here, he's got a nose just as sensitive as any dog, and he got a sniff of something on Simon—just before he disappeared. Something that might be a real clue."

I heard Willie shuffling awkwardly. I heard Wanda give a little gasp. But I kept my eyes on the lieutenant's face. It was something else!

He gaped. He looked pained. He glanced from McGurk to Mr. Cassidy, as if to say, "What *is* this?" Then he looked shocked, as if he couldn't believe his ears. Then he scowled right back at McGurk.

"A *smell*? A *clue*?"

McGurk nodded rapidly. His face was so serious that even the lieutenant had to calm down a little.

"Yes, sir."

"Well—go on then! What smell?"

McGurk sighed.

"That's just it. He can't remember. Only I read someplace that doctors can hypnotize people who can't remember details. To help them remember. And I was wondering—"

The tight skin on Lieutenant Kaspar's face (now a very deep pink) split open in a snarl. His hand shot out and a long bony finger quivered over our heads, the gold ring flashing.

"Go!" he roared. "Now!"

"But—"

"NOW!"

Wanda, Willie, and I were already on our way after the first "Now!" And after the second, even McGurk decided not to linger.

"And Patrolman Cassidy!" we heard the voice

roar. "If I even *see* these friends of yours again, so help me I'll have your shield!"

Then the door slammed.

"Wow!" said Wanda. "Was he mad!"

"Yeah," said Willie. "What you want to go kidding him about my nose for?"

"Hypnotism!" I said. "No wonder—"

"But it's *true!*" cried McGurk. "I did read it. In the paper. How this cop couldn't remember a license plate number until they'd hypnotized him."

He stopped and turned back to look at the busy scene on the vacant lot. We turned with him.

"Poor Mr. Cassidy!" said Wanda. "I think we might have got him into trouble."

The patrolman did look worried as he stood there kicking at a tuft of grass, head down.

"Poor Mr. Cassidy nothing!" snapped McGurk. "He's gonna be *proud* of us before we're through!"

"Oh?" I said. "How's that? You know a hypnotist to get to work on Willie or something?"

"No," said McGurk. "But we're going to show that lieutenant a thing or two, just the same."

"Oh, sure!" said Wanda. "They've only got that big trailer, and all that equipment, and millions of men, and truckloads of dogs. Sure we'll show them, McGurk!"

"You watch it, Officer Grieg!" growled McGurk. "Or so help me I'll have your ID card!"

It seemed to me then that it was the lieutenant who had shown *McGurk* a thing or two instead. But I wasn't about to say it aloud.

McGurk had a very determined glint in his eyes.

And when McGurk gets that look—well, you never know.

7 Willie Remembers

"So what do we do now?" I said, as we hurried along at the side of the long-striding McGurk.

"What we should have done before!" he muttered.

"What's that?"

"Go see Mr. Johnson, the paperman. Or Leo."

"What good—hey, slow down, McGurk!" said Wanda. He didn't. She had to speed up herself. "What good will *that* do?"

"He can give us the list."

"What list?"

"The list of customers on the morning route,"

said McGurk. "I mean—" Suddenly he stopped. We nearly fell over each other. "Whatever had happened to upset Simon, it must have happened on the route, Tuesday morning. Right?"

"Well—probably—yes," I agreed.

"And it had happened on that part of the route before he reached my house. Right?"

"Right," said Wanda. "Before your *street*, I'd say. Judging from the look on his face when he came around the corner—*this* corner."

I glanced around. She was right. We were at that corner now. Everything was happening so fast I hardly knew where I was. As for poor Willie, he had only just managed to catch up with us.

"Hey! Where are we going now?"

We ignored him. McGurk was talking.

"So if we go around to all the customers in this section of Simon's route, maybe one of them will be able to tell us something."

"Yes," I said. "Possibly. But won't the police have done that already?"

McGurk's lip curled.

"Huh! If you'd asked me that earlier, I'd have said yes. But now that I've seen that *lieutenant*—I wouldn't bet on it! Come on—we're wasting time."

Well, McGurk was being very unfair there. Hadn't we seen for ourselves the policemen knocking on doors the day before? But when McGurk takes a dislike to anyone he does get unfair. And his biggest dislikes are those he takes to people who give him the brush-off when he's trying really hard.

Anyway, as it turned out, we didn't even need to get hold of that list. Because—well—listen. . . .

After McGurk had said, "Come on, we're wasting time!" he set off again at the same fast pace. But he hadn't gotten more than two or three hundred yards, with Wanda and I close behind him, when Willie gave out with this yell.

"Hey! Hold it!"

We looked back. He was still near the corner where we'd stopped before. He'd stopped again, and this time he looked as if the pace had grown too fast for him.

His arms were out at his sides—quite rigid, like a scarecrow's, except for the fingers. They were fluttering like a young bird's wingtips when it wants to be fed.

Also his nose was high in the air, like a hungry young bird's beak—except instead of opening and

shutting, it was slowly rotating as he moved his neck from side to side.

"Come *on*, Willie!" snarled McGurk. "You gotta learn to keep up. Your legs are long enough. Move it!"

"Hey!" cried Willie again, fingers still fluttering, nose rotating. "No! Come back here! I—I think— yeah! *Catnip!*"

This last word came out almost like a scream.

And as it screeched out, so Willie swooped.

Now it was one of those sea-birds he reminded me of—the ones that suddenly dive into the sea to spear fishes.

Only the "sea" in this case was a big clump of shrubbery at the bottom of a driveway.

"I think he's gone nuts, I really do," murmured Wanda. "McGurk, you've driven him—"

"Nuts nothing!" growled McGurk, striding out again, but this time back toward Willie. "He's re-membered!"

And Willie *had* remembered. He must have caught a whiff of that catnip as he was hurrying to catch up with us. Maybe it was because we had disturbed the air, hurrying along so fast in front of him, causing a kind of slipstream. I don't know.

But this was *it*. This was the smell that Willie had caught coming from Simon two mornings ago. He was positive.

"Good work, Willie!" said McGurk, after bending to take a sniff himself. His own eyes were gleaming like a cat's as he turned to look up the driveway.

"So what we have to do is check that this is one of the houses where he delivered."

"No need," said Wanda. "Look!"

She was pointing to the front porch.

There, on the mat in front of the door, was a sloppily folded newspaper, lying just where Leo Johnson had tossed it.

"Right," said McGurk. "Got your notebook, Joey? This is where we make inquiries." He was already marching up to the front door, pulling out his ID card. Then he stopped at the porch steps. He pointed off to the left of the mat. "Hey! And here's *another* paper."

He was right. It too was sloppily folded.

He bent and picked up both papers.

"Yesterday's," he said. "Yesterday's *New York Times*. Here's today's—and here's *yesterday's*."

We stared at the papers, then up at the silent house, still not quite sure what it all meant.

Then McGurk said it. Slowly and menacingly.

"It looks like someone left in a hurry, men. Without bothering to cancel the papers. The day before yesterday. *The day Simon disappeared!*"

8 Grand Larceny Auto?

"Do—do you think we *should* tell the police?" whispered Wanda.

Even McGurk was looking a bit scared.

Then he tightened his lips.

"Huh!" he grunted. "Well. . . . Maybe. . . . But there's no harm in giving it just one more try. Stay back."

We didn't need to be told twice. McGurk pushed the bell. Willie was halfway back down the driveway already. Wanda and I stayed on the porch, just behind McGurk, but I noticed that Wanda was standing sideways, ready to take off. Like me.

But there was no answer—not even after the

second and third rings—so we breathed easier and looked around more carefully.

The mail hadn't been collected, either. It was still stuffed into the mailbox at the side of the door. McGurk poked at one of the envelopes jutting out.

"Perrins," he murmured, reading out the name. "I'm not sure I know—"

"They're fairly new here," said Wanda. "I know the name because Mrs. Perrins used to be an airline stewardess and that's what I always wanted to be. Before I decided—"

"All right, all right!" grumbled McGurk. "You can tell us all about your ambitions some other time, Officer Grieg. Right now we've got to try and figure out what happened between her and Simon Emmet on Tuesday."

"You think she's the 'she' he was talking about?" I asked.

"I'm getting to be more sure of it every second," said McGurk, with a glance down the yard at the clump of catnip. "Although what the trouble was I don't know. . . . What's she like, Wanda?"

"Oh, she seems all right," said Wanda. "She's got red hair all smoothed back and caught up in a knot, and she always smiles and says hi. You know. Not like some adults. And she wears—"

"What about Mr. Perrins?"

"Well, I don't see much of him. He works at the airport, in the control room or something. And—" Wanda shrugged. "That's about all, I guess."

"They don't sound like—uh—crooks—to me," I said.

"Who said anything about crooks?" said Willie.

"Well—uh—kidnapers. You know."

We gazed again at the silent house, the overflowing mailbox, the two papers, the deserted driveway, the clump of catnip.

"Could be they're smugglers," said McGurk.

"Huh?"

"Well—you know. Being connected with the airport. Maybe Simon stumbled into something, saw them unloading some smuggled drugs from the car. Maybe ducked down in the catnip there to spy on them and—why not?"

Willie and Wanda looked interested, but I was shaking my head.

"No way," I said. "Simon was more worried about someone spying on *him*, remember? Not the other way around."

"Yes," said Wanda. "But he must have been in *some* sort of contact with the clump, to be smelling of catnip like that."

"Yeah!" said Willie, nodding vigorously.

"Anyway," I said, "we can't stand here all day. What do we do now?"

McGurk shrugged.

"What *can* we do? It's just fine for Wanda to say we should tell the police, but you heard what that lieutenant said. He doesn't want to *see* us again. And—"

"Oh, *no!*" gasped Wanda, suddenly staring down the street. A small light blue car had just started to slow down. And: "Oh, yes!" she groaned, as the car turned into the driveway. "It's her!"

I could understand the tone in which she said all this. I was feeling scared, too. Scared and trapped. And I'm sure Willie was, because as soon as the car had cleared the end of the driveway and had come up by the side of the house, he started to make for the gap and the safety of the street.

"Wait!" shouted McGurk. "What's the matter with you?" Then: "Good morning, ma'am," he said. "Is this Mrs. Perrins?"

Well by then I had calmed down as well. The woman looked a bit surprised as she stepped out of the car, but not menacing. Yet she did look somehow *disturbed*. Pale. With some of the smoothed-back hair straggling out of place. And no make-up.

"Yes," she said, coming up to the porch. "Who are you?"

I think McGurk sensed the need to play it cool.

At any rate, he didn't flash his ID card. Instead, he picked up the two papers and handed them to her.

"Just friends of Simon's, ma'am," he said mildly.

His eyes were gleaming though, as he watched to see how she'd react.

She simply looked puzzled. She took the papers, thanked him, brushed a strand of hair from her eyes, and said: "Simon? Who's Simon?"

"The newsboy, ma'am," said McGurk, still watching.

This time there was a reaction.

"Oh, *him!*" she said, with an angry frown. "I suppose he's sent you to make excuses, has he? Well you can tell him from me that if it hadn't been for—"

"We can't, Mrs. Perrins," said Wanda. "We can't tell him anything. He's still missing!"

"Missing?"

The woman blinked. If she was putting on an act, it was a good one.

"Haven't you heard?" said McGurk. "He's been missing since Tuesday. The police are all over the neighborhood."

"Oh—the—the *police?*"

The woman got paler than ever. Suddenly she sat down, right there on the top step of the porch.

"You all right, ma'am?"

"Gosh . . . I didn't . . . yes . . . sure. Tell me about it. *Tuesday*, you say?"

"Yes, ma'am. . . . Excuse me, but I believe you haven't been home since then. Is that correct?"

"Yes, yes. . . . Oh heavens! Did he *say* anything? Why he was running away? I mean I suppose he *has* run away?"

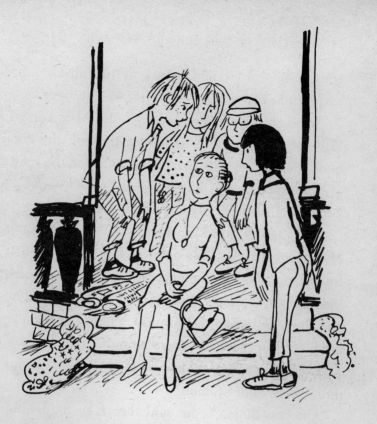

"Nothing. That's why everyone's puzzled, Mrs. Perrins," said Wanda, speaking gently. "What happened?"

"Well . . . well they can't blame *me*. I mean *can* they? I . . . well. . . ."

And so she told us, still protesting that it wasn't her fault.

It had really begun on Monday morning, not Tuesday. That was the morning when Mr. Perrins had come home from night duty at the airport very early and very sick.

"It was a wonder he made it," said Mrs. Perrins. "He collapsed as soon as he got through the door here. Luckily, there wasn't much traffic on the roads at that time. He . . . he thought it was flu *then*."

"Is he all right?" Wanda asked politely.

"He is *now*," said Mrs. Perrins. "That is, he's out of danger. But that was only the beginning of it. It turned out to be pneumonia. By late Tuesday morning he had a temperature of 105. That's when he had to be rushed to the hospital, where I've been at his bedside practically every minute since."

"Umm!" murmured McGurk. "So that's why you didn't hear about Simon?"

"Ah, yes—Simon," she said, her face hardening a little. "I was telling you about *him*. . . ."

It had been around four on Monday morning when Mr. Perrins arrived home and collapsed. For the next few hours she was busy trying to make him comfortable. Then, at about eight A.M., she happened to glance out of the bedroom window. That's when she saw the newsboy.

"John had left the car at the bottom of the drive-way. I guess it was just too much to drive even another inch. So there was the car—and there was this—this friend of yours, with the door open, peering in."

"Simon? But—"

"That's what he was doing. Then he must have seen the curtain move or something, because he looked up, saw me, and shut that door pretty fast."

"But—"

"I'm only telling you what I *saw!* Anyway, I didn't think much about it just then. Figured he was interested in how fast it would go or something. Boys usually are, aren't they? Well, anyway. *Later* that morning I decided to drive it up into the garage. John had only a foggy idea of what was happening, but he said he was sure he'd left his car keys in the ignition. But no keys. They weren't in any of his pockets, either. Luckily I have a spare set, but those particular keys of his were special and he was worried."

"Special, ma'am?"

"Yes." The woman blushed a little. "They were on a solid silver key ring I'd bought him for a wedding gift. With a valuable silver medal attached. A St. Christopher medal—you know—the special saint for—"

"Travelers," I said. "Yes, Mrs. Perrins. But about Simon. You didn't think that *he*—?"

"Well, what else was there to think? John had left his keys in the car. Then I see the boy with the door open. Then I find the keys are missing. And then *I* started worrying. I mean really worrying. There have been so many cars stolen lately."

"That's true, ma'am," said McGurk. "But—"

"I thought, what if there's a gang and they're using boys like that to look out for keys left in unlocked cars?"

"It makes sense, ma'am," said McGurk. "But—"

"And the more I thought about it, the more I worried. I mean he *looks* like an honest boy—"

"And he *is!*" said Wanda.

"But I thought, isn't that just the sort of boy a gang would use? Someone innocent-looking?" Mrs. Perrins sighed. "So I went on worrying, but keeping it all to myself because John was so sick and I knew I mustn't alarm him. I even told him I'd found the keys, just to keep him from worrying. But that didn't help me any. I lay awake all Monday night, wondering what to do. Then I decided to have it out with the boy himself."

"So you *accused* him?" I said.

"Yes, I did. I was waiting for him on Tuesday morning. John was no better and I was feeling awful. And—well—I guess I went after him. Really lit into him."

"Simon?"

"Yes. I said I didn't want any excuses. I said if the car was stolen he'd be the first suspect. And if he didn't bring those keys back before noon, I'd just have to risk upsetting my husband and—and—"

"You'd call the *police?*" said Wanda.

"Yes," said Mrs. Perrins.

"Wow!" said Willie. "No wonder—"

"No wonder Simon was so upset!" I said.

"Grand Larceny Auto!" said McGurk. "That's a terribly serious crime even to be accused of. And you couldn't have been more wrong, ma'am. Old Simon wouldn't steal a rock off your front driveway."

"He's the most honest boy in—in the world!" said Wanda.

"You—you really think so?" asked Mrs. Perrins, looking up with wide, scared eyes.

"We're *sure* so!" said McGurk.

"Anyway," I said. "*Did* you go to the police at noon, Mrs. Perrins?"

"No. John had become so much worse. I had to arrange for an ambulance to take him to the hospital. And after that I was there with him, helping him fight for his life. So I forgot about the keys and the car and everything else."

"Well, Simon didn't," said Wanda.

Mrs. Perrins nodded.

"I guess not. And look—I'm sorry. I really am. But—well—where *are* the keys? What happened to them? My husband had to have them to get here. They can't just have disappeared into thin air. Where are they?"

"That's what we mean to find out, ma'am." This time McGurk did pull out his ID card. "Do you mind if we take a look around, out here in the yard?"

9 "We reconstruct the crime!"

For what happened next, it will help if you study this plan of the Perrins's yard. I didn't have time to draw it on the spot, right then, that morning, but later I made it for the records.

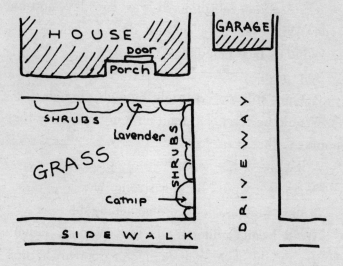

At first, after Mrs. Perrins had told us to go ahead and had gone into the house to freshen up, we were baffled. Even McGurk didn't really know where to start. In fact it was Wanda who suggested beginning with the catnip clump.

"I mean this is where the car must have been parked," she said, going to the spot. "The driver's door would be right beside it. That's why Simon would smell of it. He'd be standing *in* it, practically."

"When?" said McGurk.

"When he opened the car door, of course."

I was the first to see what was wrong with *that*.

"On *Monday* morning? It was Tuesday morning when Willie smelled it on him, don't forget."

Wanda's face clouded.

"Oh, gosh—yes."

McGurk still looked bright enough, though.

"Would he carry the smell on him for twenty-four hours, Willie?"

Willie shook his head.

"Not so's it would be *that* strong. No."

So now McGurk looked dejected again.

"What I can't understand," said Wanda, "is why Simon should have opened the car door in the first place. If he *wanted* to look at the speedometer he could have seen it through the window, surely?"

Willie broke the silence next.

"Hey! Well maybe he did take the keys at that! Maybe—huh—something came over him. When he saw the silver medal. Maybe he just couldn't resist and—"

"*Not Simon!*" We were all speaking at once as we turned on Willie. "*No! . . . Never!*"

Willie backed off, shrugging, blinking.

"He was *thoughtful!*" Wanda sighed. "Simon wouldn't do anything to cause trouble. Just the opposite. He—"

"Hah!" barked McGurk. "Wait!"

He was already making strange movements. His arm was out, twisting at the wrist. He was leaning forward into the driveway, over the catnip clump. He nearly lost his balance.

"What?" I asked.

"I'm Simon," he said. "Imagine it. I'm looking into the car. I have my hand on the door. I'm very thoughtful. I like to be helpful. What am I doing?"

"You're looking into the car," said Willie.

"I said that! But why?"

"Well," I said, "you've seen something wrong maybe."

"You bet I have!" said McGurk, still leaning forward, staring into space.

"But what?" asked Wanda. "If he'd seen a person in it, a—a car thief or something—he wouldn't have had to open the door. Anyway, Mrs. Perrins would also have seen the person."

McGurk straightened up and grinned.

"Not if the 'person' had been only one foot tall," he said.

Wanda scowled.

"McGurk," she said, "this is no joke."

He ignored her. Still grinning, he looked around from face to face.

"Like a *cat?*" he said. "Hah? I mean look. Here we are. Next to a catnip clump. Next to where the car was. Now if Mr. Perrins was so sick when he got home, he might have left the window wide open, and—"

"Or the door!" I said.

"Yes. Or even the door," said McGurk. "I mean, she didn't say she saw Simon *open* it. She said she saw him *with it open*. Right? Just check on that, Wanda, please. Go ask her. Now."

While Wanda was gone, McGurk said:

"There's another possibility, too. If the door *was* open already. Let's just take a look at the car."

We followed him up the driveway. He peered inside.

"Yes," he said. "It's got courtesy lights, all right."

"Huh?" grunted Willie.

"Lights that light up when you open a door," I said.

"Right!" McGurk nodded. "And maybe *that's* what Simon was doing. Checking to see if they were still bright. Worrying that leaving the door open had run down the battery. Ready to warn the owner about it. Being *thoughtful,* as usual."

Wanda came back.

"No. She says she didn't actually see him open it. But she assumed—"

"That's all we need to know!" said McGurk.

Quickly, he told Wanda about his theories.

Her eyes widened.

"Gosh! Yes. A cat. Or the lights, Either way, it's just what Simon would do!"

"But why didn't he tell her?" said Willie. "On Tuesday, when—"

"It sounds like she didn't give him the chance," said McGurk grimly.

"And what about the missing keys and medal?" I said.

"That," said McGurk, clapping his hands together, "is our next move, men!"

"How?"

"We reconstruct the crime," he said, going back down the driveway. "Or the *incident*—because I don't think 'crime' is the word here. . . . Look. Mr.

Perrins gets out here, right? He's so sick that he doesn't shut the door properly. Or bother to close the window. I mean he's so sick he hardly knows what he's doing. All he wants is to get in the house. So . . . he stumbles out. . . ."

And so McGurk pretended to stumble out. In fact he made such a production of it he looked like he'd been riddled with bullets. But no one criticized his acting. We were too interested in his thinking.

"He's remembered to take out the ignition keys," said McGurk, swaying about over the catnip clump. "That would be force of habit. But now he's groping about in his pockets, reaching for his door keys."

McGurk swayed and groped like he had snakes in his pockets.

"And all the time, he's staggering toward the front door."

McGurk began staggering, but still keeping up with his swaying and groping.

"The shortest route. Over the grass here."

Swaying and groping, McGurk staggered over the front lawn.

"He's probably got the car keys in one hand still. But he has a fever. The hand is slippery with sweat. And by now all he's thinking about is the other set of keys. . . . Don't you *see?*" said McGurk suddenly turning and looking at us. "Don't you see what—"

"Sure!" I cried. "He could easily have dropped the car keys without knowing it!"

"Somewhere in the grass!" said Wanda.

"Or—here—in this—" Willie sniffed—"this lavender. Right in front of the porch!"

"Right, men! In fact anywhere in a line from the catnip to the porch here. And that's where we concentrate our search. Now!"

So, while Willie combed the catnip clump and Wanda and I searched the grass, McGurk went on his hands and knees to the lavender. After five

minutes we still hadn't found anything, but we were all smelling like angels and were very optimistic still.

"You know," said Wanda, as she ran her fingers through the blades of grass, a square foot at a time, at the side of me, doing the same, "I bet Simon had thought of this himself. On Tuesday. I bet he started

to look through the catnip. But the shock was too much for him, and he panicked, and—"

"*Got 'em!*"

It was McGurk. His face was red and damp and a lavender sprig was sticking to his forehead. But his eyes shone as he held up the ring with the keys and the silver medal.

We were crowding around him at the door when he handed them to Mrs. Perrins.

"Oh! Oh, heavens! Oh, thank you!" she said. "I'm so glad to—*oh, but that poor boy!* What shall we *do?*"

"Leave it to us, ma'am," said McGurk. He turned to us. "Come on, men. We've got work to do!"

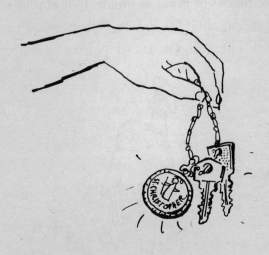

10 The Surprise Visit

"What work? Eh? Come on, McGurk. What work?"

McGurk didn't reply until we were back in our HQ. Even then he had first to rock back and forth in his chair about fifty times. But he was thinking hard; we could tell from the gleam in his eyes.

At last he spoke.

"Mrs. Perrins started all this because she didn't know Simon. Right?"

Willie shrugged. Wanda frowned. But I agreed.
"Right."

"O.K. So we're going to finish it because we *do* know Simon."

This time I joined Wanda in frowning.
"How?"

McGurk stood up. He started walking slowly around the table.

"Listen," he said. "I'm Simon—"

"Not again!" Wanda groaned.

"Yes, *again! Only this* time I'm Simon after Mrs. Perrins has accused him. Tuesday morning. And, boy, am I worried! Even Mrs. Perrins was never as worried as me." Then McGurk gave a great display of worry.

He squeezed his hands together. He frowned so hard that all his freckles seemed to merge into one big brown blotch. He chewed on his bottom lip like it was a stick of bubble gum. He rolled his eyes and he clutched at his hair.

"All right, all right!" said Wanda. "So you're worried, McGurk—"

"Simon. I'm being Simon," said McGurk.

He started chewing on his nails like he had peanut butter on them.

"All right then," said Wanda. "You're Simon. So—"

"So I'm half out of my mind!" cried McGurk. "Because although I'm hoping the keys might simply have been dropped in the yard, I can't help thinking someone really might have stolen them. Some other kid. Some kid who *was* going around stealing car keys for a gang. And that thought hits me right then, when I'm starting to look in the catnip."

He put on another great act. He bent down and pretended to be scrabbling about in an invisible clump. Then he leaped in the air like he'd found a rattlesnake and he clapped both hands to his head.

"Oh, no!" he yelled, still being Simon. "What if the car does get stolen? I really will be Number One Suspect! Grand Larceny Auto! Oh—oh—oh—what shall I do?"

Poor Willie stared at him as if he really was Simon. Poor Willie looked ready to burst into tears. But Wanda and I were cooler.

"O.K., McGurk, so what *does* Simon do?" I asked.

McGurk became himself for a few seconds.

"Simon panics," he said. "Simon is in a state of shock." He reeled about, clutching the table for support. He groaned. He twitched. He rolled up his eyes until only the whites were showing. "That's how we found him that morning, isn't it?"

"Well, not *quite* like that," said Wanda. "But go on. What happens after he's seen us?"

"He feels worse than ever. He thinks even we are

lined up against him. He feels really hunted. So he takes off. To find someplace to cool off. To think straight. To work it out. Or maybe with some crazy idea of hitching a ride all the way to Seattle to his father, because he wasn't sure his stepmother would believe him. I don't know. But what I *do* know is this." Now he was all McGurk—eyes gleaming. "I know that Simon is not a quitter."

"Oh?" said Wanda.

"No," said McGurk. "Remember his advice to you? When you were shocked after your fall? To get right back up that old tree again? Well it may have taken longer to work with him, because his shock had been such a big one. But I bet that by the time he'd spent that first night away from home, he decided to come right back and go on and finish searching that yard properly."

"So why is he still missing?" I said.

"Because of Shock Number Two. He probably snuck back just in time to see cops crawling all over the neighborhood. Maybe he overheard someone say they were searching for him. Maybe he thought it was for stealing the keys. And he's tired by now. His nerves are all on edge."

McGurk acted nervy. He twitched all over, as if he'd gotten ants in his clothes.

"So Simon panics again," he said. "Panic Number Two. He runs and hides."

"But where does he go this time?" asked Willie. "With all those people looking for him?"

"Simon? Are you kidding? He knows the whole area inside out, Willie. He didn't have any trouble setting you straight that time you were lost, huh? And don't forget, he also knows all the houses on his route where the people are on vacation. Where he can hide out in a shed or garage without being disturbed. But still he's not going to quit. Because when he isn't in shock, Simon is very, very patient."

"Patient?"

"Yes, Joey. Remember how he spent all that time unraveling your fishing line? That means he's going to have *another* try at searching the Perrins's yard. Only this time, knowing the cops are looking for him, he's going to have to be very careful."

"Yeah!" said Willie, hooked. "He'll wait until dark, right?"

"Wrong, Willie."

"But—"

"If he waits until dark he'll have to use a flashlight. And that would be just great, wouldn't it? In someone's front yard! No. What he'll do is use a disguise."

"Oh, sure!" said Wanda scornfully. "He could dress up as one of those lawn ornaments. A gnome or something!"

"Or a firefly," I said. "That way he *could* use a flashlight in the dark without getting people suspicious."

Even Willie joined in.

"Or a cop," he said. "Simon could dress up as a cop and pretend to be searching for himself—hee! hee!"

But McGurk was sure that disguise was the only method Simon could use.

"There's no other way," he said.

And he was wrong.

There *was* one other method Simon could use to look for those keys in safety. One obvious thing that not one of us thought of. No, not even I.

McGurk was just saying:

"So from now on, we stake out the Perrins's yard, and we watch out for any strangely dressed character, and—"

There came a tap at the door.

I went and opened it. At first I thought it was one of the little kids playing hide-and-go-seek. He was all crouched down on the bottom step, so that his head was below the level of the yard.

But it was no little kid.

It was Simon—white-faced, grimy, and almost as nervous-looking as McGurk had been in the middle of his act.

"Quick, let me in," he whispered. "I need your help. I'm sorry I didn't trust you the other morning. But I was in trouble. I still am. I'm being accused of stealing cars. And now you're the only ones I know who *can* help."

Then he told us how, and *that* was the one method—the only method—he could use. *Get someone else to search the yard for him!* Someone he could count on to do a good job.

We all felt so proud that he'd picked us—at last.

"You came to the right place, Simon," said McGurk, the proudest of us all. "Because you know what? The McGurk Organization is so much on the

ball, we've done it already. Even before you asked. We've searched the Perrins's yard!"

Now Simon looked almost as shocked as McGurk had in the middle of that act.

"But—but how did you know?"

McGurk ignored the question. He was bursting to say this next bit.

"And not only have we searched that yard, but we have also *found* those keys there!"

"Really? No kidding? Oh—gee!—I—when?"

We told him—the whole story of our meeting with Mrs. Perrins and our investigations.

"So now you tell us something," said McGurk, looking very wise and winking at us fellow officers. "Which of your vacationing customers' sheds or garages have you been hiding out in?"

Simon shook his head. He was so pleased that you could tell he hated to disappoint McGurk.

"Er—well—you're close, McGurk. But they weren't on vacation. As a matter of fact, I spent last night in *your* shed, Willie."

Willie gasped. We all did.

"Ours?" said Willie.

"Yes. I remembered hearing how you once used your shed to hide a cat in. You chose the shed because no one ever used it."

McGurk sighed.

"Oh, well, you can't win them all!" he said.

Simon was looking thoughtful again.

"Look, now that I'm in the clear again, I'd better call Mom. Could I use your phone, McGurk?"

"Yes, but on one condition."

"Name it," said Simon, "and you've got it."

"On condition that I get to call Lieutenant Kaspar with the news before anyone else does!"

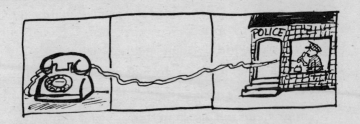

11 The Shining Trophy

And that's what happened.

As soon as Simon was through telling his step-mother that he was alive and well and ready to start back home in a few minutes, McGurk called the police. He was so pleased with this opportunity that he made me put my ear next to his, so that I could make this full record of the call for our files:

```
        TRANSCRIPT OF CALL: J.McGurk to

               Lieutenant Kaspar


DESK SERGEANT:  Yeah?

McGURK:  It's about Simon Emmet.

DESK SERGEANT:  The missing kid?  Hold on and I'll
    put you through to the Command Post. . . .
    (CLICKING NOISES). . . . O.K.  Go ahead.

McGURK:  I'd like to speak with Lieutenant Kaspar,
    please.

LIEUTENANT:  You've got him.  Who is this?
```

```
McGURK:  Jack P. McGurk, head of the McGurk
         Organization.

LIEUTENANT:  Who--oh, no! Not you again! Not the
         boy hypnotist! Not the boy hypnotist with the
         boy bloodhound! Look, sonny--I told you--
         we're busy, very busy, and--

McGURK:  You can relax now, sir. We've found him.

LIEUTENANT:  You've what?

McGURK:  Yes, sir. Thanks mainly to Officer
         Sandowsky.

LIEUTENANT:  Officer who?

McGURK:  Officer Sandowsky, sir. The one with the
         nose. He--

LIEUTENANT:  Huh! Never mind that. Where is the
         Emmet boy now?

McGURK:  Right here, sir. We thought you might like
         to know before--

LIEUTENANT:  Darned right! Don't move. Just let
         me have your address and we'll send a squad
         car right away.
```

And it came right away. Driven by Patrolman
Cassidy.

Simon looked worried.

"I promised to go straight home," he said.

Patrolman Cassidy nodded.

"That's just where I'm taking you, son. First stop."

We wanted to go along too, but the policeman
shook his head.

"Only Simon," he said. "I've got strict instructions.
Sorry, kids."

McGurk was terribly miffed.

"I *always* wanted to ride in a police car!" he said,

as we watched it go off down the street.

He was still very gloomy that afternoon, when we were busy in our HQ, tidying up our records. In fact we were beginning to get really worried about him when the knock came at the door.

"See who it is," McGurk said with a sigh.

It was Patrolman Cassidy.

"Hi!" he said, stepping in, looking very alert and pleased with himself—just the opposite of McGurk, slumped there at the end of the desk. "I've come to congratulate you all. I hear the lieutenant himself is going to do it officially, but he's busy right now."

"Yeah," grunted McGurk. "Busy riding around in squad cars, I bet!"

Mr. Cassidy blinked. Then grinned again.

"Well, anyway—I think you did a great job. All

of you. And I'd like to show my appreciation with—
uh—a little trophy."

We stared. He was pulling something metallic
and bright from an oilskin pouch. Something just as
bright as Mr. Perrins's silver key ring
and medal, but much bigger.

"Hey! Handcuffs!"
said McGurk, bright-
ening up a bit himself.

"Yeah!" said Mr. Cassidy,
his grin widening.

"*Real* handcuffs?
Real *police* handcuffs?"

Mr. Cassidy nodded.

"Complete with keys." He dangled them. "Actually it's an older pattern than the modern issue.
But they're just as good. They were my father's. He
was a cop, too."

McGurk had come forward, almost on tiptoe.

"Could—may—may I hold them?"

"Son," said Mr. Cassidy, "you may *have* them. For
the Organization. That's what I brought them for.
Like I said—a trophy."

"Gee! Mr. Cassidy!" gasped McGurk, squirming—
I mean really *squirming*—with pleasure. "You—you
shouldn't have! There was no need—"

But McGurk was holding onto them pretty tight just the same.

Yes, sir!

And now they hang on the wall behind his chair, and that jerk won't let anyone so much as touch them unless it is their turn to polish them up, which only comes around every four days for each of us.

Anyway, apart from Simon's personal thanks, the gift of the handcuffs was the best reward we could ever have dreamed of. It was so good that McGurk never even thinks any more about the missed opportunity of the squad car ride. All he hopes for now is that soon we'll get a case where we can snap those handcuffs on somebody's wrists.

Well, who knows? Where McGurk is concerned, before long we may be doing just that!